No Bullies Allowed!

Here Comes Smelly Nellie

by Teddy Slater Illustrated by Marilee Harrald-Pilz

SCHOLASTIC INC.
New York Toronto London Auckland Sydney
Mexico City New Delhi Hong Kong Buenos Aires

For Max Rodman — a great big brother.
— T. S.

For my pal Eddie.
—M. H-P.

12 11 10 9 8 7 6 5 4 3   7 8 9 10 11 12/0

Printed in the U.S.A.
First printing, January 2007

Nellie Higgenbottom was used to being teased.
After all, her name *was* Nellie Higgenbottom.

At home, her big brother Max called her Nellie Jelly . . . when he wasn't calling her Nellie Belly, that is.

But Max always smiled and ruffled her hair
when he said that.
So Nellie didn't really mind. Not much.

"Don't pay any attention to Max," Nellie's mother said.
"He's just joking."
And Nellie could tell that was true.

It was different at school, though. When Hannah Martin yelled out, "Here comes Smelly Nellie," Hannah wasn't smiling. She was laughing.

Most of the other kids laughed, too.
And they weren't laughing *with* Nellie.
They were laughing *at* her.

They laughed even harder when Harry Bing chimed in.
"You mean Smelly Nellie Belly Higgenbottom," he said.

Nellie tried to laugh, too. But she felt more like crying.
And then it seemed as if everyone had another mean
name for her.

Worst of all was "Smelly Nellie *Big*-enbottom!"

Now, Nellie's bottom wasn't very big at all.
In fact, it was just the right size for sitting on.
Nellie knew that. So did everybody else.
But no one seemed to care. *"Big*-enbottom!
Bigger-bottom! *Biggest*-bottom!" they chanted.

Nellie held back her tears. It wasn't easy. She could
hardly wait for the three o'clock bell to ring.

Nellie's mother was waiting at the bus stop.
"Hi, sweetie," she said.
Then she asked Nellie the same question she asked
every afternoon. "How was your day?"

Nellie gave the same answer she gave every afternoon.
"It was okay."
Nellie didn't say anything about the name-calling.
She was too embarrassed.

Nellie didn't want to go to school the next day. She knew her mother would let her stay home if she said she was sick. But that would be a lie. Poor Nellie didn't know what to do.

What would you do if a bully or a group of kids called you names?